The Little Sleepyhead

Fran Manushkin • illustrated by **Leonid Gore**

Dutton Children's Books • New York

For my great nephew, Benjamin Rosen Engelmann
F.M.

To all Little Sleepyheads everywhere
L.G.

Text copyright © 2004 by Fran Manushkin
Illustrations copyright © 2004 by Leonid Gore
All rights reserved.

CIP Data is available.

Published in the United States by Dutton Children's Books,
a division of Penguin Young Readers Group
345 Hudson Street, New York, New York 10014
www.penguin.com

Designed by Tim Hall · Manufactured in China
ISBN 0-525-46956-7
First Edition
10 9 8 7 6 5 4 3 2 1

A long time ago,
when the world was so young
that all the rocks were little pebbles
and all the chicks were still in their eggs,

there lived a Little Sleepyhead.
All day he played,
leaping over streams
and racing up hills
and trying to catch clouds,

but now he was tired
and needed a place to sleep.
He saw songbirds sleeping in nests

and turtles tucked into shells,
but where could *he* sleep?

"I need someplace soft,"
said the Little Sleepyhead.
The grass looked soft,
so he lay his head there.

Bugs wiggled up his nose,
and grasshoppers tickled his toes,
and he laughed and laughed.
But did he sleep?

No!
So he searched some more.
He saw beavers sleeping in ponds
and squirrels hugging branches,
and *that* looked cozy.

So the Little Sleepyhead climbed up a tree
and hugged a branch.
It was bumpy, so bumpy
that he couldn't fall asleep.

Down he climbed,
yawning and yawning,
and what did he see then?

He saw frogs floating on lily pads.
How dreamy they looked!

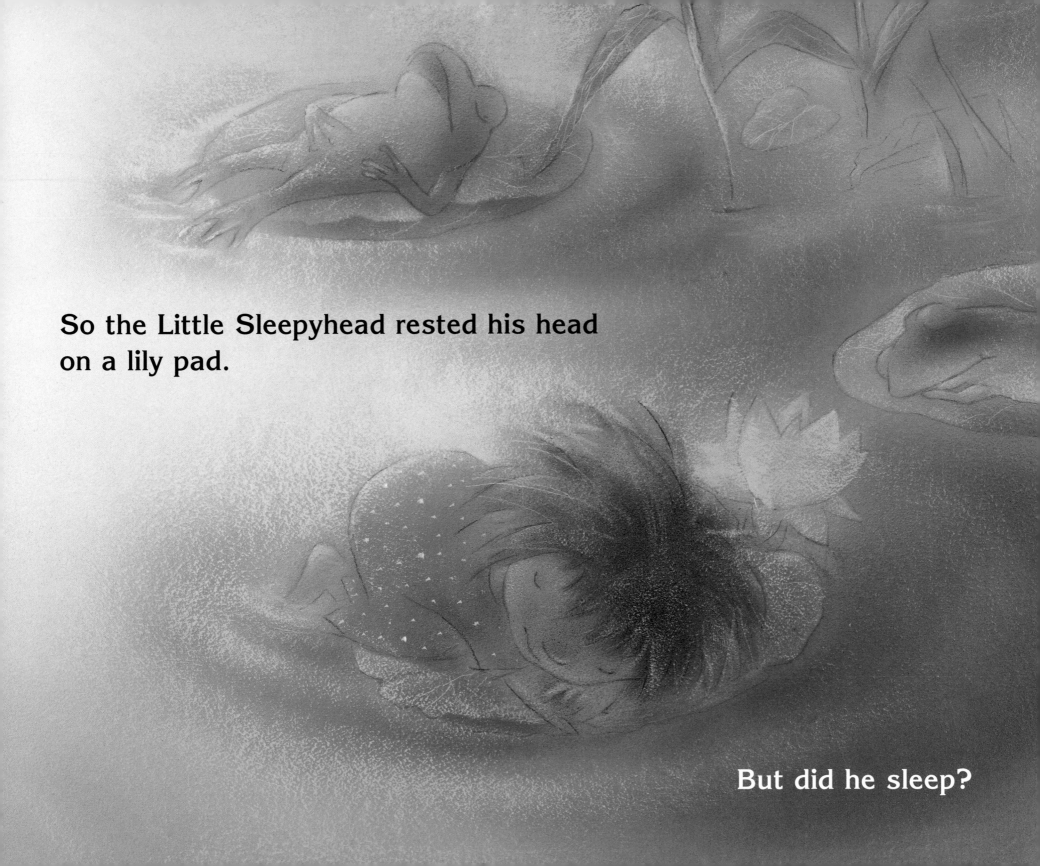

So the Little Sleepyhead rested his head
on a lily pad.

But did he sleep?

No!
The lily pad tilted
and tipped,
and *SPLASH!*

Down he sank,
  down
    down
among the glittery fish
and swaying grass . . .

until he floated up again,
sleepy and wet.
Now what could he do?

He searched some more,
and what did he find?

A bear!
That bear looked warm
and soft, so soft,
the Little Sleepyhead
rested his head on him.

But that bear began snoring, *Grrrr, grrrrr, grrrrr,* making so much noise,

the Little Sleepyhead shouted,
"SHUSH! BE QUIET!
I WANT TO SLEEP!"

His shout was so loud,
he woke everyone up!
He woke up worms in their twisty tunnels
and ducks in their dreams
and sheep in their flocks . . .

and beavers, who began busily chewing down trees.
And those trees fell down with a great big—CRRASH!

That crash startled the birds,
who ruffled and shook their feathers,

and those tickly feathers made the wind sneeze,
AH-CHOO! AH-CHOO!
And it blew those feathers around and around,

and they landed dreamily in a soft, high heap.
"*This* is what I need!" said the Little Sleepyhead.
"*A bed!*"

Quick as a wink,
he snuggled into the soft, warm feathers,
curled up, and closed his sleepy eyes.
But did he sleep?

No!
He opened his eyes
and looked around.
Something is missing, he thought.

"*Baa!*" A little lamb came along.

The Little Sleepyhead held out his arms,
and she snuggled inside them.

"*This* is what I need—someone to hug!"
said the Little Sleepyhead.
He closed his eyes,
but did he sleep?

YES!

And if *you* have a bed,
and something to hug,
then *you* can go to sleep, too!